TIMMY TURNER,
ACTION HERO

BASED ON THE TELEPLAY BY **BUTCH HARTMAN**
AND **STEVE** ~~~~
ADAPTED BY M~~~~
ILLUSTRATED BY ~~~~

D1509817

Simon Spotlight/Nickelodeon
New York   London   Toronto   Sydney

PROLOGUE

I am the Crimson Chin, the mightiest superhero in the universe!

I am known by many names. The Scarlet Defender of Chincinatti. The Mandible of Might. The Jaw of Justice. I'm the guy who put the *man* in *mandible*! You may also know me as the most powerful dude to ever put on red tights and fight for truth, justice, and all that other really important stuff.

The deeds of the Crimson Chin are many. And every single one is fantastic, if I do say so myself!

As the sworn protector of Chincinatti, I put my jaw on the line for justice. My big, pearly-white teeth bite so deep into crime that they leave a mark! Evildoers who've felt the molars of the Crimson Chin know that this hero means business.

But even I, the amazing Crimson Chin, can feel a shiver of dread now and then. Yes, even the bravest of the brave can quake in fear when faced with a truly awesome, unbeatable foe. Why, believe it or not, even I can feel a little bit queasy once in a while.

Queasy is just how I felt the time I faced my greatest challenge. With pecs flexed and a cleft as hard as granite and as deep as the Grand Canyon, I fought the hardest fight of my superhero supercareer.

On that fateful day I met villains more clever

than an Albert Einstein action figure! I faced foes so fearsome that even a cute, cuddly little teddy bear could not stop their tide of destruction. On that day I battled enemies so cruel they made a little girl cry—and you can't get any worse than that, let me tell you!

But in the end, with the help of a brave little boy named Timmy Turner, good triumphed over evil!

Ah, yes. I remember that day as if it were yesterday. Hmm, I think it *was* yesterday . . . and a warm, sunny Saturday morning at that. Everything looked peaceful, but don't let *that* fool you! Some really bad stuff was about to happen. . . .

CHAPTER 1

"Almost ready!" yelled A.J.

Chester, Timmy Turner, and A.J. were playing in Timmy's backyard. It was Saturday, which meant no school. Even better, the sun was shining.

Junk was scattered all over the grass. While Chester and Timmy watched, A.J. tied a rusty old bucket to a wooden broom handle. Then he stuck the end of the broom into the middle of a big metal spring and tied it on with rope.

Finally, with Chester's help, A.J. pulled the stick back until the spring was stretched as tight as it could get. Then he tied it back with another piece of rope. "It's ready to fire," A.J. said proudly of their newly created catapult.

"I'm ready too. I have my slingshot and a bunch

of stones," said Timmy. "We can launch stuff into the backyard with the catapult, and I can use my slingshot to blast it."

"Prepare to load the catapult!" A.J. yelled.

"Load it with what?" asked Chester with a frown.

For a long time, no one said a word. Then Timmy snapped his fingers. "I've got it!" he cried. "Let's blow up our old stuff!"

"That's a great idea," laughed A.J. "I have lots of old science stuff at home."

Timmy, A.J., and Chester hurried off to get their old stuff. Later, when the boys met up under the tree, they had a whole bunch of junk that was just waiting to be smashed!

"I'll load the catapult," said A.J. He dumped Chester's pink teddy bear into the bucket, then gave Timmy a thumbs-up.

Timmy loaded his slingshot with a stone and got in position.

"Pull!" Timmy commanded.

With a tug on the string, A.J. fired the catapult. The stuffed teddy bear flew high into the air until it almost touched the treetops.

Then Timmy fired his slingshot and the bear exploded. *Thwack!* A shower of fluffy cotton stuffing rained down on them.

"It's raining bear guts!" marveled Chester.

"Hooray!" yelled A.J. "Let's do it again."

This time A.J. loaded an Albert Einstein action figure into the bucket. The little doll looked like an old man with gray hair, bushy eyebrows, and a funny moustache.

Timmy lifted his slingshot and aimed into the distance. "Pull!" he yelled.

Albert Einstein spoke his last action phrase: "*E* equals *MC* squared." Then he flew into the air and was blasted to pieces!

Timmy, Chester, and A.J. cheered as bits of plastic fell from the sky.

"Bye, Albert," said A.J. with a wave.

"This sure was a great idea, Timmy," said Chester. "Hey," he cried. "Let's launch my retainer."

"Yeah!" said A.J. He snatched the retainer out of Chester's hand and loaded it into the catapult.

"Now that we're ten, we don't need our dumb nine-year-old stuff!" said A.J. Then he tugged the rope. The boys cheered as the retainer flew over a wooden fence and out of sight.

"Hey," said Timmy as he held up a bright red superhero doll. "Let's launch this!"

Chester was shocked. "But Timmy, that's your favorite Crimson Chin action figure! You can't launch that!" he gasped.

"He even has eighteen chin-tastic action phrases!" A.J. cried.

A.J. touched the button on the Crimson Chin's

chest. "Quick, to the hydrofoil!" the action figure commanded.

Timmy made a face. "But it's last year's model. I am so beyond his lame phrases."

Timmy got ready to drop the Crimson Chin doll into the catapult. He was about to launch the Scarlet Defender of Chincinatti into the air when a horrible noise interrupted him.

"Timmy? Timmy?" screamed a little girl.

"Oh, no!" Timmy cried.

Fearing the worst, Chester raised a pair of binoculars to his eyes and scanned the area. He spied a little girl in pigtails. She wore great big glasses. Her mouth was open in a loud yell—so wide that Chester could see her braces sparkling in the sunlight. The girl gripped a photo of Timmy Turner in one hand. Worst of all, she was coming toward them!

"Run for your lives!" Chester howled. "It's Vicky's little sister, Tootie!"

CHAPTER 2

"Quick! To the antigirl fortress," yelled Timmy, pointing to the wooden tree house at the other end of the yard.

The rickety old structure was nestled on two branches high up among the leaves. A rope-and-wood ladder hanging from the door was the only way inside.

The boys raced across the yard and scrambled up the ladder as fast as they could.

But they were too late! Tootie had spotted them. "Tiiiiimmy!" she hollered.

Timmy was in a panic. Tootie was getting closer! Timmy knew that she liked him, but he thought she was yucky! "Timmy! Wait for me!" yelled Tootie.

The boys climbed even faster.

Inside the tree house Cosmo and Wanda, Timmy's godparents, were floating in a glass fishbowl disguised as goldfish. When they heard the commotion outside, the fairies nodded their heads and waved their magic wands.

With a *poof!* the tree house was instantly transformed. Splintery wooden walls became computers. Posters turned into electronic view screens. Wooden barrels and crates became high-tech command chairs with real cup holders!

The sliding doors opened with a swish. Timmy, A.J., and Chester raced into the control center and took their positions. A.J. manned the view screens. Chester armed the weapons system.

Still clutching his Crimson Chin action figure, Timmy sat in the command chair in the center of the room. As he hopped into the seat, Timmy pressed a red button on the armrest. Out popped Wanda and Cosmo, still inside their fishbowl and still looking like goldfish. No one, not even Timmy's best friends, could know about his fairy godparents.

A.J. twirled a dial. "Enemy on screen, Captain," he announced. An image of Tootie appeared on a large-screen television, even bigger than life. She still gripped the picture of Timmy. But now the photo was soggy from all the wet, slobbery kisses she had showered on it.

Timmy saw the image on the screen and shuddered. Then he held his Crimson Chin action figure high above his head.

"Prepare to fire phasers!" ordered Timmy.

Chester pressed a button. A giant slingshot popped out of the tree house window. The band was stretched tight, ready to fire.

"Phasers locked, Captain," said Chester grimly.

Inside the fishbowl, Cosmo's eyes bugged out. "I love when the phasers get locked," he cried.

On the television screen, Tootie was yelling.

"Tiiiiimmy! Can I come up and play?"

"Fire!" Timmy commanded.

Chester pressed the launch button. With a *boing,* the slingshot let loose. A big red water balloon flew at Tootie. At the last second the balloon stopped in midair. It spun around over Tootie's head, then burst. Instantly Tootie was soaked with cold water.

"Waaa!" Tootie howled. "I'm so wet, you can't even see how much I'm crying!"

Up in the tree house, the boys cheered.

Tootie, still shrieking, looked up at them. "Can I at least come up and dry off?" she cried.

But Timmy showed Tootie no mercy. After Chester automatically reloaded the slingshot, Timmy yelled out another command.

"Fire!"

This time Tootie saw the balloon coming. When it paused in flight to spin over her head, she stepped out from under it.

Unfortunately for Tootie, Cosmo and Wanda had made these water balloons magical. The balloon moved over Tootie's head, then exploded with a *splat*. "Waaa! Waaa!" sobbed Tootie, dripping wet.

"Yeah!" cheered Timmy, Chester, and A.J. as they slapped palms in a high five.

But their celebration was interrupted by an urgent beeping. The sound was coming from the slingshot control panel.

"Darn it!" said Chester. "We're all out of balloons!"

A.J. grinned. "Let's go get some more, and we

can strap the Crimson Chin down to one!"

Timmy looked at his action figure. "Yeah!" he said with a big smile. "We can hit Tootie with a balloon *and* a plastic doll!"

"Waaaaa!" Tootie howled from outside.

A.J. and Chester raced for the exit.

Timmy's friends were gone, and now he was alone with his action figure.

"Well, I guess this is good-bye," Timmy said to the Crimson Chin. Then he pressed the button on the Chin's plastic chest.

"You're my best pal!" the action figure said.

Timmy's smile vanished. Suddenly he felt bad about trashing his once-favorite toy.

Just then Cosmo and Wanda turned back into fairies and floated out of their fishbowl. "If you used to like it so much, why are you going to destroy it?" Cosmo asked.

Timmy shrugged. "Because I don't need this doll anymore. I have you guys!" Then Timmy gave the Crimson Chin a second look. "Still, he *was* pretty cool," Timmy admitted.

Wanda and Cosmo smiled at each other. They knew exactly what Timmy was going to say!

"You know," Timmy said, "I wish I could play with him one more time."

Wanda fired a magical bolt at Timmy, and Cosmo directed his magical energy at the Crimson Chin action figure.

Poof! Poof!

"Hey!" squeaked Timmy in a tiny voice. "I'm toy-size!"

Then the Crimson Chin doll landed right next to Timmy, who was still seated on the now-giant command chair.

"There's evil afoot! I mean, a-chin!" bellowed the Crimson Chin in a bold, manly voice.

"Wow!" said Timmy, his eyes wide. "You made him come alive!"

"Sure," Cosmo replied. "Sitting next to a lifeless doll would have been boring."

Suddenly the Crimson Chin lifted his cleft in

alarm. "Some horror approaches!" he warned, pointing to the window. Timmy spied Tootie lurking outside.

The Crimson Chin snatched up Timmy in his massive arms. "Quick! To the Chin Cave!" the red-clad hero cried.

Leaping off the chair, the action-packed action figure landed on a skateboard. Still clutching the helpless, toy-size Timmy, the Crimson Chin zoomed through a secret escape hatch and was gone.

Tootie was coming in, and Wanda and Cosmo were trapped in the tree house. At first they didn't know what to do. But when Tootie pounded on the door, the two fairies turned themselves into plastic fairy godparent action figures.

The door swished open and in walked Tootie. "Timmy! Where are you?" she screamed.

Then Tootie saw Cosmo and Wanda, who were lying motionless on Timmy's command chair.

"Neat! Fairy dolls," Tootie declared. "I can add Timmy's dolls to my Timmy love shrine collection."

Tootie snatched up Wanda and Cosmo.

"Maybe if you took us to your house, Timmy would follow you and try to get us back!" said Cosmo.

Wanda shot him a stern look.

"What?" Cosmo whined. "Can't I have an action phrase too?"

"That's a great idea!" said Tootie.

Still clutching Cosmo and Wanda, Tootie raced out of the tree house, down the ladder, and all the way home.

CHAPTER 3

Seconds after Tootie left the tree house, the secret escape hatch opened again. Out flew the Chin and Timmy.

Timmy looked around but saw no sign of his fairy godparents.

"The commissioner is missing," said the Chin. His words didn't make sense, but then again most of the Crimson Chin's action phrases didn't.

While Timmy searched for Cosmo and Wanda, the Chin struck a pose and flexed his muscles.

"Look at the size of these pecs!" he cried. But Timmy wasn't paying attention. He was worried about Wanda and Cosmo.

"Help me find them, Chin!" Timmy begged.

The Crimson Chin struck another heroic pose.

Then he leaped out the window. As Timmy watched, Chin raced into the branches and was lost among the leaves.

Then Timmy saw Tootie racing across the yard with Wanda and Cosmo gripped in her hand.

"Oh, no!" cried Timmy. "I'm stuck toy-size and my fairy godparents are being taken to Vicky's house! There's only one thing to do!"

In a panic, Timmy dropped to the floor and began sucking his thumb.

At that moment, A.J. and Chester returned with more balloons. Timmy heard them coming up the ladder, but he didn't want them to see him doll-size. Timmy froze, his thumb planted in his mouth, pretending to be a plastic doll.

"Wow!" Chester exclaimed. "A Timmy Turner action figure. With thumb-sucking action!"

"What should we do with it?" A.J. asked.

Chester scratched his head. "Well, it is an uncanny likeness of our best friend. Let's launch it into Mrs. O'Leary's yard!"

A.J. peeked out the tree house window to the yard next door. There were beehives scattered all over the property. Big bumblebees with huge stingers circled the hives.

"You mean the lady with the pet bees?" A.J. cried. "We can't do that!"

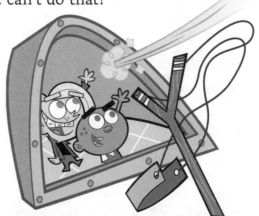

Chester dipped the toy-size Timmy into a big, sticky pot of honey!

A.J. grinned. "Now we can do it!" he cried.

Before Timmy could stop them, Chester loaded him into the giant slingshot. *Whoosh!* Just like the helpless Albert Einstein action figure, Timmy flew into the air at an amazing speed!

"Aaaaaaaaaa!" Timmy screamed as he flew over the fence into Mrs. O'Leary's yard.

Timmy wanted to close his eyes, but he was too scared. So instead he watched helplessly as he hurtled toward the beehives and the angry bees that buzzed around them. . . .

While Timmy Turner streaked toward certain doom, the Crimson Chin had problems of his own. He'd leaped through the tree house window and into the tree only to land in the lap of an angry squirrel!

"Give up now, villain! Or face the full brunt of my chin-tastic power!" demanded the Crimson Chin.

But the squirrel was guarding a stash of acorns and wouldn't budge.

"If it's a fight you want, then so be it," the action figure declared as he leaped on the squirrel's back. The little creature tried to throw the Crimson Chin off its back, but the avenger hung on tight.

Finally, with an angry squeak, the squirrel threw the Chin aside and tried to run away.

"Not so fast, evildoer," the Chin declared. "My jaws are clenched in the name of justice!"

With acorns scattering everywhere, the Crimson Chin tackled his furry foe. Using his legendary leg-lock leverage, the scarlet action figure finally trapped the helpless squirrel in a headlock.

Things were bad all over.

Stuck pretending to be toys, the fairies were trapped in Tootie's bedroom. They watched in awe as Tootie played in front of her shrine to Timmy.

On the center of Tootie's dresser was a school photograph of Timmy. The picture was surrounded by burning candles and incense. In the center of the room was a life-size statue of Timmy.

Tootie sat on the floor next to her toy tree house with Cosmo and Wanda by her side.

"Now I have two of Timmy's dolls to add to my Timmy collection!" Tootie chirped.

Behind her was a stack of stuff—old toys, a sneaker, a shirt. All of these things had once belonged to Timmy.

"Wow!" said a wide-eyed Wanda. "She really has a crush on Timmy!"

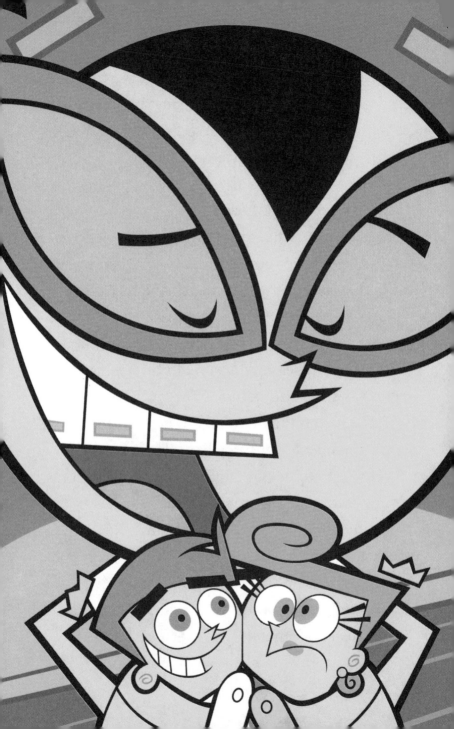

Tootie reached for her plastic tree house. "Let's play Timmy and Tootie in their jungle home," she began.

"You're me!" Tootie said to Wanda. Then she reached for Cosmo. "And you're Timmy."

Then Tootie slammed the two fairies together, mashing their faces into each other.

"Mwah! Mwah!" Tootie said, her lips puckered. "I love you, Tootie! Mwah! Mwah! Mwah! Mwah!"

Soon Wanda's head was spinning. But Cosmo had a big grin on his goofy face.

"Hey! I like this game!" he declared.

CHAPTER 4

Timmy, covered with sweet, sticky honey, was hurtling toward Mrs. O'Leary's beehives.

"Aaaaaaa! I'm dead!" howled Timmy.

Looking away from his epic battle against the squirrel, the Crimson Chin listened for more cries for help. He didn't have long to wait.

"Aaaaaaa!" yelled Timmy.

"Did somebody say 'justice'?" the Chin asked.

"Aaaaaaaa!" Timmy screamed again.

Finally the super action figure spied Timmy flying toward the beehives. The Chin also saw the bees waiting for Timmy to land, their stingers ready to strike!

Releasing the squirrel from his iron grip, the Chin leaped into the sky. Like a streak of pure crimson heroism, the Scarlet Defender of Chincinatti plucked Timmy out of the air before the swarm of bees could sting him.

Angry at being robbed of their prey, the bees launched an attack against the Crimson Chin. Timmy was still cradled in the Chin's strong grip. He closed his eyes and waited for doom.

"Evildoers, where is thy sting?" demanded the Crimson Chin.

He found out a moment later, when one of the bees stung him in the butt!

"Exercise is a great way to improve your day!" the Chin cried. Then he spun around in midair and drop-kicked the bee back into its hive.

"Point!" the Chin announced victoriously.

When they saw what happened to the first bee, the rest of the swarm flew away in panic.

Seconds later Timmy and his action-figure pal slammed into a wooden fence. Timmy bounced across the lawn and landed on his butt. The Crimson Chin's head got stuck in the fence.

"Wow! Thanks, Crimson Chin!" Timmy said. "You totally saved me. I wonder why I got so bored with you."

The Crimson Chin thrust out his jaw and spoke another of his action phrases.

"Check out my dimple! It's huge," he declared.

Timmy frowned. "Now I remember. Your action phrases stink!"

Then Timmy began to run toward Tootie's house.

"Come on," he called over his shoulder. "We have to rescue Cosmo and Wanda!"

"I eat evil for breakfast!" the Crimson Chin cried. Using his amazing rocket power, he burst out of the wooden fence and followed Timmy.

Together they were off to rescue Timmy's fairy godparents!

Meanwhile Tootie was still in her bedroom, laughing and playing with her brand-new Wanda and Cosmo dolls.

"Mwah! Mwah!" said Tootie, mashing the fairies' faces together.

Then in the middle of a pretend kiss, she suddenly pulled the dolls apart.

"Well, you're just a dumb girl," Tootie said, holding up the Cosmo doll and pretending to be Timmy.

Then, she held up the Wanda doll. "That's okay, Timmy!" Tootie said, pretending to be a grown-up Tootie. "I'll wait for you forever!"

"Fine!" said Tootie in her Timmy voice. "I'll be over here throwing water balloons at you!"

With that, Tootie picked up a squirt gun and, pretending to be Timmy, aimed the water gun at Wanda. *Splach!* "This doesn't seem like a lot of fun," said a dripping Wanda.

"Are you nuts?" answered Cosmo with a silly grin. "I'm having a blast! And look how clean you are."

Meanwhile, down in the yard, Vicky—Tootie's older sister and Timmy Turner's babysitter—was getting ready to work. The hedge trimmers and lawn mower were out.

"It's time to do my chores," she announced.

Then the mean teenage babysitter turned and came face-to-face with two terrified ten-year-old boys.

"You, trim my hedges! You, cut my lawn!" Vicky commanded.

"But these are *your* chores!" said one boy.

Vicky grinned and held up two photos. "And these are high-definition photos of you two sneaking into an R-rated movie!" Vicky shot back.

The boys quaked in fear as Vicky pointed to the tools.

"Aaaaaaaand . . . action!" Vicky shouted.

As the boys went to work Vicky crossed the sunny patio to the picnic table, where a pitcher of lemonade and a tall icy glass awaited her.

"Whew!" said Vicky as she wiped her forehead. "All this blackmailing is making me thirsty."

But before Vicky could taste her first sip, she heard the sound of Tootie's giggles.

"What?" Vicky cried.

She looked up. Through the second-floor window, Vicky spied Tootie in her bedroom. Tootie was playing and laughing and having lots of fun.

Vicky stamped her foot angrily.

"My dorky little sister is laughing when she should be down here doing my chores! Well, I'll fix that!" Vicky said, fuming. Still carrying her glass of lemonade, she stormed into the house to put a stop to all the laughter.

When Vicky was gone, Timmy and the Crimson Chin stepped out from behind a clump of weeds.

"Quick—while she's distracted! We've got to get into that house!" said Timmy.

"I have goats in my pants!" declared the Crimson Chin.

"Uh, okay . . . come on," said Timmy.

But as the toy-size boy raced from his hiding place, he felt the ground under his tiny feet begin to quake. *Rrrrr!* "Oh, no!" Timmy cried, just as the lawn mower came surging out of the tall grass. Its blade whirled, and bits of green grass flew every which way.

"Run!" screamed Timmy.

But when he turned to flee, Timmy tripped over something in the grass and fell flat on his face.

Timmy was stuck right in the middle of the roaring machine's path!

The rumble of the lawn mower got louder and louder. When Timmy looked up again, the machine was so close that he was about to be run over.

Worst of all, there was absolutely nothing he could do about it!

CHAPTER 5

Timmy, still on the ground, watched the giant lawn mower coming closer and closer. The earth trembled under Timmy's toy-size feet, and blades of grass filled the air. Only then did Timmy see the thing that had tripped him.

The object was round and pink, with sharp steel jutting out of all sides. Though the day was sunny and warm, the device was still wet with slimy drool.

"Hey, that's Chester's retainer," said Timmy. He looked up at the tall fence, and the catapult and tree house that seemed so very far away.

"Man," Timmy exclaimed, "that sure got some distance!"

Then the roar of the lawn mower battered

Timmy's ears until he could hear nothing else. The machine was just inches away from running him over!

Whoosh! The Crimson Chin dropped out of the sky in a blur of scarlet. He landed, legs braced, between Timmy and the weed-gobbling machine. "Without gravity, we'd float into space!" the scarlet avenger bellowed.

Using his amazing flex-action arm, the Crimson Chin grabbed the retainer.

"Justice, thy name is Chin!" the red-clad hero cried. Then he hurled the dental device into the rotating lawn mower blades!

As the metal retainer tangled around the spinning propellers, the boy pushing the machine saw the lawn mower spark and smoke. Then it bucked in his hand and began to vibrate.

Leaping backward, the boy watched as the lawn mower exploded, throwing chunks of smoking metal everywhere.

"All finished!" he called over his shoulder as he took off for home.

Pieces of the blasted lawn mower continued to drop out of the sky, but down in the grass the smoke was beginning to clear. Timmy rose and faced the scarlet action figure.

"Good thinking, Chin!" he said gratefully.

The Chin struck a dramatic pose. "Of all my muscles, my brain is one of them!" the Chin said proudly.

Remembering their mission, the two took off toward Tootie's house. As they trotted along, Timmy reached up and patted the action figure on the back.

"You're a cooler doll than I thought," said Timmy.

"Together, nothing can stop us!"

But suddenly a dark shadow fell over them, blocking out the sun. Timmy and the Chin slammed right into what seemed like two furry telephone poles. Then they heard a savage, canine growl.

"Grrrrrrrrrrrrrr . . ."

"Aaaa!" cried Timmy. "It's Vicky's dog!"

Doidle, the dog, glared at the boy and the action figure. Then he showed his fangs in a mean snarl.

"Grrrrrrrrrrrrr . . ."

Before Timmy could stop him, Doidle snatched up the cherry-red action figure in his powerful jaws.

Turning around, the dog scampered for home with Timmy Turner racing behind. In one powerful leap, Doidle burst through the doggie door and into Tootie and Vicky's kitchen.

"Chin! Chin! Are you okay?" Timmy yelled after them.

But if the heroic action figure heard his little toy-size sidekick calling his name, the mighty Crimson Chin did not reply.

Just then Vicky burst into Tootie's room while she was playing with Wanda and Cosmo.

"Well, well, well," purred Vicky.

Before Tootie could stop her, Vicky snatched the fairy godparents.

"What's this?" Vicky asked. "Two new toys? Well guess who they get to meet!"

Behind her thick glasses, Tootie's eyes bugged out.

"Not Mr. Hammer!" Tootie squealed.

"Mr. Hammer?" Cosmo and Wanda said, puzzled.

"Yes," hissed Vicky. "Mr. Hammer! And his friend, Mrs. Saw!"

Vicky shook a hammer in Wanda's face. Then she thrust the sharp teeth of a saw against Cosmo's neck.

But instead of acting afraid, Cosmo just grinned and introduced himself. "Hi, Mrs. Saw," he said. "I'm Cosmo, and this is Wanda!"

Wanda looked annoyed at Cosmo.

"Don't you want to be a good host?" Cosmo asked.

Vicky dropped the two fairies onto her workbench. Then she raised the hammer and saw.

"No!" Tootie yelled. She tugged on her sister's arm, trying to stop Vicky from breaking the toys. "Those are Timmy's dolls!" Tootie cried.

"Oh, that changes everything," Vicky cooed. She slipped on a metal mask and struck a match. Holding up a blowtorch, Vicky lit the gas. A flame exploded out of the nozzle with a loud *whoosh*!

With a cruel smile, Vicky placed the hot, hissing, yellow flame under Cosmo's nose.

"Hey, Mr. Fire," Cosmo said with a polite smile. "Have you met Wanda?"

CHAPTER 6

Meanwhile, down in the kitchen, the Crimson Chin was fighting a major dog-versus-action-figure battle!

Using his jawbone power, the Crimson Chin tried to free himself from Doidle's mouth. Though the Mandible of Might's amazing cleft action had put the Bronze Kneecap to rest, it did nothing to halt Doidle's vicious, slobbering attack.

Next the Chin tried using his super grip to pry himself loose. This technique had worked to defeat the Copper Cranium and his amazing wrecking-ball skull—not to mention the villainous Iron Lung and his sucking and blowing action!

Unfortunately, the Chin's martial arts moves couldn't stop Doidle. The dog kept on chewing and drooling all over the Chin. No matter what he tried, the Chin was trapped.

Just then tiny Timmy Turner burst through the dog door. "Oh, no! The Crimson Chin is being torn apart!" cried Timmy.

Timmy searched for something to stop Doidle. He spotted the glass of lemonade that Vicky had left on the countertop. "If I can dump that drink on Doidle, he might just run away!" said Timmy. "But how do I get all the way up there?"

Timmy saw a mousetrap in the corner. Suddenly he remembered the catapult he, A.J., and Chester had made that morning.

"Yeah! That'll work," said Timmy.

He raced to the mousetrap and hopped on. Timmy used his hat to knock the piece of cheese from the trap, springing it. The trap snapped, launching Timmy high into the air and over Doidle's head.

"Oof!" said Timmy as he landed on the counter. He got up and peeked from behind the glass. Doidle sat on the floor below, still gripping the Chin.

Pushing with all his strength, Timmy toppled

the glass over the edge of the counter.

"Chew on your butt, not my friend!" yelled Timmy.

The cold yellow lemonade soaked the surprised dog. Then the glass shattered on the hard kitchen floor. With a yelp, Doidle dropped the action figure.

Vicky was just about to melt Cosmo with her blowtorch when she heard the sound of breaking glass. "What was that?" she asked.

Vicky pushed Tootie aside and dropped the blowtorch. Then she hurried downstairs to investigate.

Vicky's eyes went wide when she saw the mess on the kitchen floor. There was a big yellow puddle, and her dog Doidle stood in the middle of it.

"Bad dog!" Vicky barked. "You know you're only supposed to do that outside—or at Timmy's house!"

Vicky grabbed Doidle by the collar and tossed him into the backyard. Then Vicky stormed off. After she was gone, Timmy hurried over to the Crimson Chin's side.

The action figure was a mess! Each limb was bent at an awkward angle.

"Chin! Chin! Speak to me!" Timmy begged.

Head twisted to one side, the Chin opened his massive jaws and tried to speak. No sound came out.

Timmy shook his broken buddy. "I'm sorry I got you into this mess!" said Timmy. "I promise I'll never let anything hurt you again."

Slowly the Chin turned his battered head. Eyes closed, the hero again tried to talk.

Timmy watched helplessly as the Crimson Chin struggled to speak.

"You're . . . you're . . . you're . . . you're . . ."

Finally Timmy gave his doll a good slap on the head.

"Ow!" yelped the Chin. His eyes flew open and the Chin saw Timmy standing over him.

"You're my best pal!" the Chin told Timmy.

CHAPTER 7

With Tootie and Vicky distracted, Cosmo and Wanda now had the opportunity to escape. They wanted to find Timmy before he got in too much trouble.

With a *poof!* the two fairies vanished from Tootie's bedroom and instantly appeared downstairs in the kitchen.

Timmy was there, still toy-size. He was standing over a really messed-up action figure covered in dog spit.

Timmy felt their magical presence. He looked up to see his godparents floating over his head.

"Cosmo! Wanda!" Timmy said, smiling in relief. "I wish I were normal-size!"

Two magic wands waved through the air, and

with a *poof!* Timmy became normal again.

Then Cosmo and Wanda turned and raced for the front door. "Come on, Timmy!" Cosmo cried. "Let's get you and your doll out of here."

Timmy was cradling the broken action figure in his arms.

"He's my friend. And I should have treated him better," Timmy said softly.

Meanwhile Tootie was looking all over the house for her Cosmo and Wanda dolls. When she couldn't find them, she figured her sister must have stolen them. Tootie ran down to the kitchen to find Vicky, but her big sister was gone.

When they saw Tootie coming, Cosmo and Wanda vanished.

Timmy hid too. He ducked around the corner, just out of sight, in a spot where he could watch Tootie.

As Tootie hurried into the kitchen, tears were falling from behind her big glasses. "No! No!" Tootie sobbed. "Vicky's stolen Timmy's dolls and I can't find them anywhere!" She ran around in circles, pulling at her pigtails.

"Now Timmy will never come over!" Tootie wailed. "And he'll never like me! Why doesn't he like me? Waaaaaaaa!"

Tootie threw herself on the living room couch and sobbed.

Wanda and Cosmo appeared at Timmy's side.

Wanda looked at Tootie and frowned.

"Maybe the Crimson Chin is not the only one you should treat better," Wanda said.

"You know," said Cosmo, "she might be creepy, but she does have to put up with Vicky more than you do."

Timmy nodded. "Yeah, you're right. I guess when Vicky isn't torturing me at my house, she's torturing Tootie here. That's gotta be worse."

Timmy Turner took a deep breath, stepped out of his hiding place, and walked up to Tootie.

Tootie was crying so much that she didn't notice Timmy was there.

"Uh . . . hi, Tootie," Timmy said softly.

Tootie looked up. When she saw Timmy, a big smile chased away her tears.

"Timmy! Hi!"

Tootie jumped off the couch and ran up to Timmy to hug him.

"I . . . wait!" Tootie said, pulling back when she saw Wanda and Cosmo in Timmy's hands. Then Tootie crossed her arms and glared at Timmy.

"You're only here to take back your dolls and then hit me with another water balloon!" Tootie declared.

But Timmy hung his head in shame. "Actually," Timmy said, "I wanted to say I'm sorry I was mean to you. You see, I'm just . . . I'm just . . ."

Timmy paused, searching for the right words.

"A stupid ten-year-old boy!" said Cosmo and Wanda in their doll voices.

"Right!" said Timmy with a nod. "And since I'm a ten-year-old boy, I'm not interested in girls. And I won't be until . . ."

"He's a stupid eleven-year-old boy!" said Wanda and Cosmo.

"Yeah, what they said," Timmy told Tootie.

"Then . . . there's hope?" whispered Tootie in amazement.

Her face lit up brighter than the sheen on archvillain Copper Cranium's armor. She jumped up and down, clapping her hands in glee. "There's hope! There's hope!" Tootie sang as she danced around the living room.

Timmy whispered into Cosmo's and Wanda's

ears. "I should do something nice for her. To make up, you know?"

Wanda and Cosmo both nodded.

"She's not mean," Timmy continued. "She's just a girl. It's not her fault."

At that moment, the battered Crimson Chin action figure stood up tall and proud—well, as tall and proud as a little action figure with bent arms and legs could manage.

"I'm totally into the idea of you giving me to Tootie," said the Crimson Chin. "This way, she'll always have a little piece of you she can smother and choke with love!"

"Wow!" said Timmy, scratching his head. "That was an oddly specific action phrase."

Then Timmy got a little choked up. He reached down and gently picked up his once-favorite action figure. Timmy gazed at the Crimson Chin through moist eyes. "I'm gonna miss you, pal," said Timmy.

The Crimson Chin struck a heroic pose and grinned up at Timmy. "I put the *man* in *mandible*!" the Scarlet Defender of Chincinatti said boldly.

Then Timmy turned to face Tootie. She was still bouncing happily around the room.

"Tootie, I want you to have this," said Timmy, presenting her with the Crimson Chin doll. "More importantly, I want you to have this and never, ever, ever follow me home again."

Tootie smiled and cradled the Crimson Chin doll in her arms, hugging it tight.

"Oh, Timmy," Tootie gushed. "This is the best gift ever!"

Timmy leaned close to Tootie and whispered into her ear. "And it will be our little secret of love . . ." he said softly.

Stars filled Tootie's eyes, and she saw visions of hearts and flowers and a big wedding cake. With a sigh she fell to the ground, still clutching the Crimson Chin doll to her heart.

The wonderful moment was ruined when a mean and nasty voice filled the living room.

"Now!" said Vicky. "Where was I?"

CHAPTER 8

"Aaaaa!" screamed Timmy when he heard Vicky's voice. "Evil babysitter! Gotta go! Bye!"

As Timmy ran out the door with Wanda and Cosmo in hand, Vicky came around the corner. She saw Tootie lying on the floor, the Crimson Chin doll in her arms.

"Wow!" Vicky exclaimed. "Another toy. When it rains, it melts!"

Vicky snatched the action figure away from Tootie and pulled out her trusty blowtorch. With a hiss, the flame blasted out of the nozzle.

"No! Nooooo!" Tootie howled.

Outside, the sound of Tootie's screams stopped Timmy in his tracks. He raced back to her house and peeked through the door.

He saw that Tootie was crying, and that Vicky was just about to melt his crimson pal. Turning to his fairy godparents, Timmy made the fastest wish of his life.

"I wish the Chin doll was indestructible and had twelve thousand 'I hate Vicky' action phrases!" he cried.

With a wave of their magic wands and big grins on their faces, Cosmo and Wanda instantly granted Timmy's wish.

Laughing cruelly, Vicky held the fire to the Crimson Chin doll. But instead of melting, the action figure looked Vicky in the eye and spoke.

"Your icky, redheaded yuckiness cannot pierce the shield of Tootie's love!" said the Crimson Chin.

"Ahhhh!" screamed Vicky in frustration. She held up the plastic figure with tongs and blasted it with fire once again. When the smoke cleared,. the Crimson Chin doll was unhurt.

"Evil babysitters make boy bands say 'ew'!" roared the Crimson Chin.

Vicky flamed him yet again. And again the Crimson Chin just shrugged it off.

"Why won't this toy break?" howled Vicky as she burned the action figure again and again.

Outside, Timmy turned to his fairy godparents. "I've had enough of this," he said. "I wish I were back at the tree house."

With a wave of their magic wands, Wanda and Cosmo whisked Timmy away.

Poof! Timmy appeared inside the tree house.

Floating over his head, Wanda looked down at Timmy. Her eyes sparkled with pride. "That was really sweet of you, Timmy," she told him.

"Yeah, well, as long as Chester and A.J. don't ever find out about me being nice to a girl, I'm safe . . ."

Just then Timmy heard his friends calling.

"Hey, Timmy," yelled Chester.

"Look who's here," said A.J.

Nervously, Timmy peeked out the window—and could not believe his eyes.

Down in his yard, Tootie was waving at him.

"Timmy! Timmy!" Tootie called.

Tootie was pulling a little red wagon behind her. Inside the wagon was a gigantic wedding cake. The Crimson Chin stood tall and proud on the very top of the cake. A girl doll with pigtails and funny glasses stood next to the Chin.

Next to Tootie and her cake, A.J. and Chester

were laughing at Tootie's show of affection.

"Look!" cried Tootie, pointing to the Crimson Chin doll. "This doll is you . . . and this doll is me."

Then Tootie pulled the dolls off the cake and mashed their faces together again and again.

"Mwah! Mwah! Mwah! Mwah!" Tootie gushed. "I love you, Timmy! Mwah! Mwah! Mwah! Mwah! I love you too, Tootie. Mwah! Mwah!"

"Har, har, har," laughed A.J. and Chester.

In the tree house window, an embarrassed Timmy tried to duck out of sight. But before he could hide, Tootie called to him again.

"Oh, Timmy," she yelled. "I got you something, too!"

A red water balloon sailed through the window and burst right over Timmy's head!

"You know what?" said Timmy as he shook the water off. "Love stinks!"

Wanda and Cosmo started to chuckle. A.J. and Chester were laughing, and so was Tootie. Finally even Timmy, who was soaking wet, started to laugh.

Only the Crimson Chin refused to chuckle. Instead the Scarlet Defender of Chincinatti, the Mandible of Might, the Jaw of Justice stood tall and proud and cried out in a bold and ringing voice:

"Brush your cleft every day!"

ABOUT THE AUTHOR

Marc Cerasini has written thirty books for children including the movie novelization books for *The SpongeBob SquarePants Movie, Eloise at the Plaza*, and *The Adventures of Jimmy Neutron, Boy Genius*. He's also written books featuring *Teenage Mutant Ninja Turtles, Totally Spies!,* and *The Fairly OddParents*. Marc lives in New York City with his wife, Alice, his ten cats, and way too many action figures.

ABOUT THE ILLUSTRATOR

Thomas LaPadula has been an illustrator for more than twenty years and has illustrated over forty children's books, including books based on *The Adventures of Jimmy Neutron, Boy Genius* and *The Fairly OddParents*. Tom graduated from Parsons School of Design with a BFA, earned his MFA from Syracuse University, and teaches illustration at Pratt Institute.